Published by Inhabit Media Inc.
www.inhabitmedia.com

Inhabit Media Inc. (Iqaluit), P.O. Box 11125, Iqaluit, Nunavut, X0A 1H0
(Toronto), 146A Orchard View Blvd., Toronto, Ontario, M4R 1C3

Editors: Neil Christopher and Louise Flaherty
Art director: Danny Christopher

We acknowledge the support of the Canada Council for the Arts for our publishing program.

We acknowledge the support of the Government of Canada through the Department of Canadian Heritage Canada Book Fund program.

Printed in Canada

Library and Archives Canada Cataloguing in Publication

Qitsualik-Tinsley, Rachel, 1953-, author
Skraelings : clashes in the old Arctic / Rachel and Sean Qitsualik-Tinsley.

ISBN 978-1-927095-54-6 (pbk.)

1. Inuit--Juvenile fiction. I. Qitsualik-Tinsley, Sean, 1969-, author II. Title.

PS8633.I88S57 2013 jC813'.6 C2013-908382-0

Canadian Heritage Patrimoine canadien

Canada Council for the Arts Conseil des Arts du Canada

SKRAELINGS

Rachel and Sean
Qitsualik-Tinsley

1

Unknown Places

Here's the story of a young man who, at the time of his tale, had no clue where his family might be living. If you had been there to ask, the best answer he might have given is:

"Somewhere behind me."

Not that he was lost. No, it was simply that happiness means different things to different people—and it was his great joy to travel across strange lands. He went without human companionship. He had no idea where he was going. There were no enemies in his life. No friends (except maybe his sled dogs). Yet not one of these facts meant that he was lost.

Unknown places, even uncertainty about where he would next sleep or eat, rarely frightened the young hunter. You, however, whoever you are reading this, would have scared him. Not because you have two heads, or you're coloured green, or you come from another planet. No, it's exactly because you come from the same planet as him that you might have scared this person.

You see, you are from another *time*. On our

earth, the earth that you know, the world is choked with people. We can see them on TV. Sit with them on an airplane. Brush shoulders with them in busy halls or on the street. Unless you're very lucky, you don't know what quiet is. Real silence. Not the quiet you get when folks stop yammering. We're talking about the silence of standing alone in the wide Arctic—on the great Land—where only the wind or an odd raven whispers from time to time, and the loudest sound is your own breath.

That kind of quiet has a heaviness to it. A life of its own, you might say. And that is the sort of quiet our hunter was used to.

This is not to say that you couldn't have been friends with the young man, since he was very much a human being, like yourself. It is simply that, even if, by some magic, you could have spoken a common language with him, your ideas of the world would have been very different. To be honest, the easy part would have been explaining televisions and airplanes to him. Even busy halls and streets. But how would you have gotten across the simple idea of a country? Or a border? In our world, the earth is so crowded. There are so many rules. It's normal that everyone knows their citizenship. You can barely move without a passport. And you can't step on a clot of land that hasn't been measured and assessed for its value. It would be strange to hear of land that isn't owned. Every inch of dirt, in our time, belongs to somebody. In our world, people even talk about who should own the moon.

But the young hunter's land was not just dirt, you see. It was not land with a little "l": something we can measure and pretend to own. His was the Land. And he called it *Nuna*. And like everything under the Sky, it had a life of its own.

Land as property would have made the young man and his relatives laugh. After all, the Nuna was a mystery. No one knew its entire shape or extent. Humanity did not set limits on the Land. The Land set limits on humanity. It was the Land, including the sea that bordered it, that made demands on how all life existed.

"No one can even control the Land," Kannujaq might have told you, "so how can one own it?"

That was the young hunter's name, by the way: Kannujaq. He was named for a mysterious stuff that came from the Land. In his language, *kannujaq* described a funny, reddish material. It was rare, but known to a few of his people. You probably would have recognized it, called it "copper," and tried to tell Kannujaq that it was a metal—but that would have meant very little to him. You see, a tiny bit of copper was the only metal he had ever seen. You might have then tried to explain to this young hunter that he only thought copper was special because he lived in the Arctic, and so long ago.

But we almost forgot: you can't tell Kannujaq anything. It would be over a thousand years before we could write about Kannujaq, much less let you read about him. And no matter how hard Kannujaq dreamed, he could never have imagined people like us.

In Kannujaq's time and place, he was usually too busy to dream, anyway. The Land never let his mind wander for long, holding him in an eternal moment. To this day, it has that power, the ability to force the mind into a single point of attention. Visit it sometime. Find a place away from "progress." Maybe you'll see why the Land was such a beloved mystery to Kannujaq and his folk. While you're on the Nuna, stand on a windswept ridge. Raise your arms, open to the grand Sky. And imagine how Kannujaq stood.

Kannujaq's eyes were closed, his nostrils pulling in the pure air, and the silence was such that he seemed to detect every stirring in his world. A raven muttered, and he opened his eyes to spot one on a nearby, lichen-encrusted boulder. Another wheeled in the sky above him. He smiled, knowing that the birds resented his presence, and his eyes panned over the rocky ridges that played out before him. The low slopes mixed shades of brown, a bit of purple, some bits of dark green from heather and willows that grew no higher than his knee. In the troughs between the slopes, the low valleys, there was barely enough snow for his dogsled. By now, he was soaked with sweat. Long tongues dangled from the mouths of his exhausted dogs.

Kannujaq's smile eventually faded. Though the Land had rarely frightened him, he experienced a shiver of dread.

Here and there on the most distant ridges, Kannujaq spotted *inuksuit*—stacks of flat stones, carefully piled so as to resemble people when their silhouettes were viewed against the sky. And Kannujaq knew who had made them. His grandfather had said so. The inuksuit were the works of *Tuniit*, a shy and bizarre folk who had occupied the Land long before the arrival of Kannujaq's family. It was said that the strength of the Tuniit was great. Hauling a stone the size of Kannujaq himself was as nothing to one of them. That was just as well, since the Tuniit relied on stones to hunt. Since the inuksuit resembled people standing on the hills, caribou took paths to avoid them. Every year, when the caribou did so, the Tuniit supposedly took advantage of their route, herding the animals into zones where they could be slaughtered. The Tuniit hunted with bows, as Kannujaq's own people did. Kannujaq's grandfather had seen one of the Tuniit hunting sites: all bones on top of bones. Some new. Others quite old. It had seemed clear that the Tuniit had hunted in their weird way for generations.

Kannujaq frowned, recalling his grandfather's stories, and not even the Land's glory was able to pull his thoughts away from the Tuniit. He wondered about the Tuniit hunting style. It meant that they stayed in pretty much the same place. Maybe even year round. That was a strange notion to Kannujaq. His people were always travelling, exploring for exploration's sake, family members splintering off to found their own little groups along new coasts. For generations, travel, a hunger for the unseen, had been the great drive of his folk. Ringed seals. Lovely whales. Stinky walruses. All the creatures of the coasts—these made up food and tools to fuel a search whose sole purpose was life itself. Life was a joy, and one grand hunt.

The Tuniit, thought Kannujaq, *who could survive their way?* He was not cold. But, in thinking about these not-quite-human folk, a chill ran through him. He stood alone in their hunting lands. He had come to regret taking this detour. His winding path among the hills had led him away from the coast, where he was most comfortable, and his dog team was having a rough time among the rocks.

He sighed and started back down to his sled, when a low howl made its way over the wind. In a moment, it was joined by another. Then several more. Eventually, the howls were like those of a small pack of wolves. Even a large pack would have been nothing to fear—Kannujaq was armed with a bow and a spear, both crafted according to the high standards of his people. And then there were his dogs to defend him. But Kannujaq nevertheless shuddered at the sounds ahead of him: he knew all animal noises, and these cries were not those of true wolves.

Tuniit, he thought, *imitating wolves. Maybe driving caribou.*

So, even now, the Tuniit were hunting in this place. He decided not to bother them—or chance being bothered by them—slipping and sliding his way back down the slope, to where his dogs awaited. Luckily, his team was only making low, anxious whining noises at the wolf sounds of the Tuniit. But if Kannujaq did not get his dogs out of here, it would be only a matter of time before one or more would howl in return.

Soon, the sled was again making its slow way back toward the coast, rushing ahead on the occasional patch of snow: sticking, rushing ahead, sticking again. Kannujaq was young, as strong as any other youth he had ever known, but this part of the Land was wearing him down.

Much time passed, and, despite the tongues waggling from their heads with overexertion, Kannujaq noticed that his dogs were growing excited, ears standing high on their heads. He was more attuned to their body language than to what lay under his own fingernails. It took him a moment to realize that the dogs were smelling a camp ahead—maybe a source of food and rest. Kannujaq was fond of the idea, since a storm was moving in and the light snowfall interfered with his distance vision. Fortunately, the days were growing long, so there was still enough light for Kannujaq to spot twisting lines of smoke in the distance, where the ground levelled out.

Kannujaq grinned, pleased to see several figures approaching from out of the snowfall. Camp folk. He began to urge his dogs forward, but paused.

Something bothered him about this place.

Dogs, he thought to himself. *I don't see any.*

Kannujaq was familiar with the kind of camps he had grown up in, all temporary, as established by his ever-roaming family. He had even seen a few camps set up by distant relations, usually using interconnected rib bones, from the skeletons of whales scattered along the shores, as shelter. Normally, any camp would be full of dogs, which were used for hauling pack-loads in the summer and sledding in the other seasons. The sight of a place without any dog teams made Kannujaq uneasy. It was like coming across a community without people. Then he spotted one loose dog out of the corner of his eye, and felt a bit better.

That dog, he thought, *where's it off to?* As he watched, squinting, the animal disappeared into the haze of thickening snowfall.

Kannujaq was startled by an odd noise. A thin cry. He turned back toward the approaching figures, the camp dwellers he had first spotted. He grinned, getting ready to raise his arms in greeting.

His grin quickly faded as he realized that they had not stopped to greet him.

They were running at him.

And they looked nothing like Kannujaq's folk.

2

Place of Murder

In a single moment, all of the strange facts of this place came together—and the word "Tuniit" flashed through Kannujaq's mind.

There was no time to reach his bow. He could only think to fumble about for his spear. Kannujaq had never before seen one of the Tuniit—a single *Tuniq*. Despite the fact that his elders had described them as "almost people," his imagination had pictured them with fangs and claws. As if they were as much wolf as human. Instead, as their faces came into sight, Kannujaq was shocked to see how human they looked. Their features were round, dark with the soot they were said to burn instead of seal oil (for which they were also called Sooty Ones). But their faces were human. It seemed that Kannujaq was looking at a mixed group of Tuniit men, women, and children, dark faces twisted up in fear. Some were carrying babies, awkwardly, in their arms. The men and women among them were marked by odd hair styles. Both had great lengths of hair twisted up tightly, but the men wore theirs in a peculiar ball on top of their heads. The women wore their hair in clusters over each temple.

All they shared in common were their shabby, sooty tops. Their bear-fur pants. Their short, squat frames.

No wonder, Kannujaq thought to himself, *there are so few dogs here*. Maybe it was that he'd been so tired, worried about making it back to the coast, finding someplace to rest—but one way or another, he had stumbled into a Tuniit camp. He, like his dogs, had assumed that this was a human encampment. Instead of avoiding the Tuniit, he had walked straight into them. Such a mistake! Now he would probably end up ripped apart by Tuniit. With the thoughts that came to him in his panic, he imagined his own corpse. Lying in pieces. Pulled at by these creatures who were half-human, half-animal. The Tuniit could haul boulders as if they were pebbles.

What would Kannujaq look like after they had grabbed him?

But the Tuniit did not attack. All at once, the whole group seemed to catch sight of Kannujaq. All, males and females alike, ground to a halt. It was as though they'd been startled by the sight of him. Then, as though they shared one mind, the Tuniit turned and ran in a different direction.

Fleeing, Kannujaq realized. *From me*. Then, his heart still pounding in his chest, his eyes watching the figures disappear back into the haze, he thought some more.

But they were already running before I got here, he thought. *What would make Tuniit run?*

Then Kannujaq realized that he had made a mistake: Not all of the Tuniit had fled. They had left behind one small, hooded person. It was impossible to see if it was a boy or girl. If the lone figure had been human, like Kannujaq's folk, he or she would have been tall enough to be a child on the edge of young adulthood. Not quite old enough to take on adult duties.

Then the wind blew at the child's hood, and Kannujaq became sure that he was seeing a boy. So human in looks! Far from being afraid, the boy was smiling, and seemed riveted to the sight of Kannujaq's dog team.

Kannujaq decided to take a risk. He stepped forward, raising his arms to show that he meant no harm. Maybe a human greeting would be understandable even to a Tuniq.

Kannujaq half expected the boy to run, though the youth surprised him by actually moving closer. He began to babble excitedly, but Kannujaq had some difficulty understanding the words. It was almost normal language, but different—a kind of Tuniit talk. Strangest of all, the boy kept grinning from the depths of his vast hood, which concealed much of his sooty face.

The boy kept pointing at Kannujaq. In a few moments, Kannujaq seemed to grasp what he was saying: The lad was actually glad that Kannujaq had come. Also, he was late? The boy had expected him? They were here. Them. Those Ones had also arrived. There were other words, as well, words Kannujaq couldn't quite make out. And there was one word that the boy kept repeating, but it was no use—Kannujaq simply couldn't understand all of what the boy was saying.

Kannujaq did, however, realize that the boy was not pointing at him. The lad was rambling about the necklace around Kannujaq's neck. On it were strung claws from Kannujaq's first bear, along with a special bit of stuff that his grandmother had given him. In fact, Kannujaq was named for that very stuff. On his necklace was a reddish-brown loop of kannujaq. It was all that remained of a needle passed down by Kannujaq's ancestors. And it was said to have been used by his great-great-grandmother, who had lived in lands without name, back in the times before Kannujaq's family did so much exploring.

It was also said that, in the old days, people sometimes took the kannujaq from rocks, grinding it to sharpness with other stones. It didn't hold a fine edge like some materials—such as jade or flint or ivory—but it lasted a long time, and some people liked the fact that it could be easily re-sharpened. On top of it all, the kannujaq was pretty to look at. Kannujaq himself liked the look of it, and he often rubbed his own thin loop between thumb and forefinger, until its shine reminded him of the sun setting on the water.

The boy, for whatever reason, seemed obsessed with the kannujaq.

With gentle touches at his arm, the boy began to lead Kannujaq into the Tuniit camp. There was something desperate about the lad. Something that made Kannujaq want to indulge him. As they went, the boy's grin faded, and his pronunciations became impossible to understand. Increasingly, his tone became emotional, even a bit crazy, until his babbling trickled off like an ice-choked stream. Stiffly, Kannujaq forced one foot in front of the other, somehow feeling more child-like than the one he followed.

It's a dream, he thought for a moment. *Has to be. I'm dreaming I'm with Tuniit. And I'm asleep*.

But Kannujaq had never before dreamed the touch of cold wind on his cheeks. He had never dreamed of detail. Curling snowfall. Stones underfoot. The sound of his own breath. The weather alone would not let him remain convinced that this was fantasy. It was getting worse. Quick, sharp gusts were whipping crystal snow particles about like sand. Whenever the wind eased off for a moment, Kannujaq could see a squat figure or two: Tuniit, like before, running as though for their very lives.

Sometimes Kannujaq stiffened, startled by different voices.

Screaming.

After a few moments, he spotted a row of seven glowing fires—the peculiar way in which Tuniit kept their cooking fires—lined up outside of an enclosure of flat rocks, about waist-high. The weird boy led him around it, slightly downhill, toward the shore. When the snow was not stinging his eyes, Kannujaq could see the corners and walls of other stone dwellings. He could also see . . .

Death?

On the ground were several dark heaps—the bodies of fallen Tuniit. The boy led Kannujaq, stumbling, past the dead. Corpses lay about the place like so many seals dragged up from the shore. The Tuniit grounds were all bare stones. No old snow or ice. And wherever Kannujaq's eyes rested for longer than a heartbeat, he could see new, wind-driven snowflakes becoming caught on rocks. Sticky with dark blood. Already freezing. The boy began to lead him more quickly. Other details were lost to him, but Kannujaq had spotted enough for his thoughts to whisper:

Murder. Place of murder, this is . . .

Kannujaq swallowed. His mouth and throat had gone dry. He should have turned back as soon as he'd seen that this was a Tuniit encampment! If they were involved in a feud with some other community, he wanted no part in it. Kannujaq pulled his arm away from the boy. He turned around, looking for his dogs.

The boy's hand clamped down on his wrist, and the lad yanked at Kannujaq with all his strength. The boy was not strong enough to move him, but Kannujaq still froze in shock, momentarily forgetting his panic. No one had ever dared to touch him in such a way. No adult. No child. Among his own folk, physical attacks occurred only between the most terrible enemies—never openly. To Kannujaq's family, violence equalled madness.

But these aren't people, he remembered. And at

least they're not tearing me apart.

Then Kannujaq frowned in thought. The boy's strength didn't seem all that unusual. In fact, it seemed about like the brawn of a human boy around the same age.

Kannujaq was distracted by shouts from the beach. The voices were like those of men, but the roars were fierce. Threatening. Like those of animals. Kannujaq realized that living Tuniit were now passing him and the boy. Some were staggering, barely noticing either. Many Tuniit were kneeling on the ground, weeping over their dead in a too-human way.

As though suddenly realizing that he'd offended him, the boy released Kannujaq. Again, the lad babbled out his odd words. One word in particular. A word that Kannujaq had not been able to understand.

Then Kannujaq got it!

Help, Kannujaq realized. *He's asking for help.*

The boy repeated himself one more time, pointing toward the beach, then ran to the side of a staggering Tuniq.

Kannujaq was finally alone. He could easily disappear. Go back to his dogs. Forget about this awful place. But he had been jarred out of his panic. He was, after all, an explorer. His fear had been replaced with curiosity.

Boy, he thought, *wants my help. How does one help Tuniit?*

He approached the shore.

3

Giants

After a moment in which the wind arose in an especially strong gust, Kannujaq could almost see the beach past the falling snow. There were fires down there. Figures moved about. Two, maybe. Three? Kannujaq realized that they were running toward the water. But something was wrong. The figures were not short and stocky, like the Tuniit.

They were huge.

Giants! Kannujaq thought, breath halting in his chest. *Monsters!*

As though his body had taken over, doing the thinking for him, Kannujaq reflexively crouched. There were giants down by the beach! They were manlike, certainly, but enormous in size, as though their mothers had become too friendly with bears. Kannujaq couldn't believe that, only a minute ago, he had been afraid of the Tuniit ripping him apart. In his fear he now seemed to hear his own heart like a drum in his ears. Thankfully, the monster-men had not spotted him.

Then the snowfall eased off. The wind died. And Kannujaq almost fell backwards at the sight of what he witnessed by the water's edge. The giants were nothing in comparison to what he was now seeing. Nothing at all.

Loon, Kannujaq thought, staring at the outline of a massive bird that rested in the waters by the shore. *Giant loon*. In comparison, the enormous bird made the giants seem tiny.

Then Kannujaq squinted, his sense for the shape and movement of animals dismissing any notion that he was looking at a living thing.

Boat, he thought.

But what a boat! Certainly, it was a bit loon-like in shape: dark and majestic in its curves. Yet it was larger than a sled. Larger than a tent or a whale-rib shelter or the iglu domes that Kannujaq's folk built in coldest wintertime. It was three times the size, maybe larger, of an *umiaq*—the skin and driftwood boats in which some families travelled from coast to coast.

On its loon-like "back" danced several swirling flames. Torches. And among these fires, there strode a single, manlike being, whose strange features instantly made Kannujaq label him the Glaring One. As the other giants scrambled up onto the back of the boat, this being turned toward Kannujaq, revealing a face that shone like the sun. In the light of the torches, the flat features glared like daylight upon waves. Kannujaq hunkered down, crouching lower, though he was fairly certain that the Glaring One could not actually see him.

One of the giants approached this Glaring One, and the tone of an argument was unmistakable. The giant pointed to the sky, emphasizing, among his other words, sounds like: "elulang" or "helulan." The weird sounds of the giant language made Kannujaq think of *tuurngait*—spirits of the Land—who were supposed to speak a strange tongue that only special people understood. Nevertheless, the gestures of the giants seemed like the same ones all men used in discussing weather. Were their words, then, their terms for the *Sila*, Sky, which was worsening by the moment? Or were they instead talking about the Nuna, Land, the shore which they wanted to leave?

The longer Kannujaq watched and listened, the less like monsters the giants seemed to him. He suspected that he was looking at very large men.

The Glaring One began to holler at the other giant, pointing to any clearer patches of sky that he seemed able to find.

Glaring One, Kannujaq thought, grunting to himself, *is the one who wants to stay.*

Then the Glaring One shoved the giant backward, as one who fails to control his temper might abuse a dog. The other giants, by now, had clambered onto the "loon"—most certainly an enormous boat. Kannujaq watched as they heaved great oars around, maybe preparing to push off from the beach. The sight of the oars snapped Kannujaq out of his terror, and he raised himself up a bit, acting less like a frightened animal, to get a better view. He wondered, now, why he had ever thought that he was looking at a loon. It was simply that the boat had a stylized prow. It was nothing like a bird. Perhaps the giants had been thinking of a beast when they had carved it. Maybe a wolf.

Now he was certain that the giants were human, tall men, given the appearance of even greater size by layers of fur and tools strapped to every part of their bodies. If they were not human beings, they were something close, like the Tuniit. What little of their skin that could be seen seemed pale. Like a corpse. The lower halves of their faces were covered in thick beards, coloured like the tan and brown fur on some of Kannujaq's dogs. A few, for whatever reason, seemed to be wearing bowls on their heads.

Kannujaq counted eight of them.

With fear overpowered by amazement, Kannujaq stepped closer as the boat left the shore, the men at the oars turning it about as though they were used to working as a team. All the while, Kannujaq studied the Glaring One, who did not row like the others, but stood over the other eight like a hunter over his dog team. Before that monstrous boat was at last obscured by the haze of snowfall, the shining face turned once more back toward Kannujaq. And while he thought it unlikely that the master of the boat could see him, Kannujaq could not help feeling as though the wide, dark eyes of the Glaring One were fixed on his own. It dawned on him, then, that this, too, was simply another man. Kannujaq clutched at his own necklace, realizing that the shining face was very much like the kannujaq stuff that made up the loop his grandmother had given him.

A mask, he thought to himself. *Their leader wears a mask. Made of kannujaq.*

The realization did little to comfort him. The owl-like appearance of that mask was raising the hair on the back of his neck. According to the ways of Kannujaq's folk, every person had animals that were friends, protectors, good signs for them in bad times. A few had enemy animals, as well. The ptarmigan had always been Kannujaq's friend. But the owl was his traditional enemy.

An owl, Kannujaq thought. *That one, he's like a great big owl.*

Had the Glaring One and his followers raided the camp? Is that why the boy had wanted Kannujaq's help? Kannujaq gulped at the thought, staring at the place where the boat had been.

He was unsure of what, or who, these men were, but he had a feeling there was no helping anyone against them. Unless it was to advise flight.

Where is that boy?

Kannujaq found the lad nearby, weeping over a fallen Tuniq, a youth who had perhaps been a friend.

A dead person is not very much like a seal, after all, Kannujaq thought.

Somewhat sickened, refusing to look toward the sounds of other Tuniit weeping around him, Kannujaq stood over the boy, who no longer seemed to register his presence. None of the other Tuniit even seemed to realize that Kannujaq was there. Respectfully, he tried to keep his eyes averted from the dead.

Kannujaq regarded the weeping boy for some

time, watching sooty tears drip from his chin. He was seeing the boy in a new light. The lad was somehow more real, not at all a character from dream, as he had at first seemed. Kannujaq's eyes followed trails of tears down the sides of the boy's neck, and spotted a partially-covered necklace of raven skulls. Among Kannujaq's own people, the necklace was something an *angakkuq*—a shaman—might wear. Here, it might simply be a boy's strange ornament. After all, the Tuniit were weird.

But they're almost human, Kannujaq thought. *Almost*.

Then Kannujaq blinked, thinking. For the first time, it occurred to him that the Tuniit might actually *be* human. Why had he believed them to be half-animal in the first place? Because his own folk had convinced him of it?

He hunkered down next to the lad; and, as he watched this mourning boy, who had wasted his time in hoping for assistance against the Glaring One, Kannujaq felt tears well in his own eyes. He had not even bothered to ask the boy's name.

Why would someone murder like this? he wondered. *Why all this violence?*

"What is your name?" he asked the boy.

Instead of answering, the lad wiped his face against the back of his sleeve, turned to Kannujaq as though noticing him for the first time. He fully removed his hood.

A chill ran through Kannujaq.

Such eyes!

The boy's eyes were as blue as deep ice. Kannujaq had never even heard that eyes could be blue, much less stared into a pair of them.

Kannujaq suddenly understood. The raven skulls. The boy's odd behaviour. The eyes. All were the marks of a special person. Someone who could see the unseen world. Maybe even understand the speech of spirits. This boy was an angakkuq.

A shaman.

4

The Unseen World

So, do you still think you could have explained your world, your time, to poor Kannujaq? Just look at the man: Even blue eyes upset him! In truth, you should have a bit of pity for Kannujaq; for, as odd as things had been up until now, they were about to get stranger.

The boy's name turned out to be Siku, meaning "ice." He had been named for the ice-blue colour of his eyes. He was indeed the resident shaman in this camp. The boy himself didn't seem to make much of this, but simply walked Kannujaq to a nearby shelter. Kannujaq had heard that a shaman was a shaman in any place or time, and that his own folk and the Tuniit were the same in this way. If so, was he endangering himself by openly befriending the boy? It seemed that the answer would depend entirely on the boy's personal reputation.

All of the shamans were feared, to a greater or lesser extent, since they could see and interact with a world that few normal people accessed. It was a world of invisible creatures. Whole populations with their own languages and traditions. Beings that were sometimes close to human. At other times, far from that, and pretty scary. It was a world of power, but one that could also consume whomever tried to use that power. It was the other side of the Land. The *Nunaup Sannginiga*. This was the "Strength of the Land," which ran like unseen rivers through the normal world.

Could such ideas make sense? Maybe. Maybe not. Perhaps they could never make sense to anyone but a shaman. Kannujaq himself barely understood what a shaman was—and he had grown up with them. But these were the simple facts: a shaman was not exactly a religious person. Nor a wizard. Nor a wise person. Nor a philosopher or tradesperson or prophet. Yet the job combined bits of all those things.

One way or another, shamans could do things, and one never knew what kind of doing a shaman did until it was done. One of them might heal. Another might make a person sick. One might inform the camp of something useful. Another might play nasty tricks. And every shaman was odd. Without exception. The community was lucky if its shaman was content to hunt and rear a family in peace.

Fortunately, it was a good bet that Siku was the only shaman here—shamans were jealous, and did not like to share territory with one another. It occurred to Kannujaq, in his meagre knowledge of how these things worked, that Siku was probably powerful. After all, it was rare to find a child shaman. They were said to be quite Strong. Not in the sense that they had muscles! No, children were Strong with the Strength of the Land. And Siku's eyes could be interpreted as a sign of such Strength. It was not simply that his eyes were blue. It was because he was different—and different people were usually important.

Who, Kannujaq wondered, *had taught the lad? Or had the Land itself somehow made him a shaman?*

The Glaring One and his men had left a terrible mess. There were bodies to gather up. Homes to restore. People to comfort. Kannujaq was led past an old man who knelt alongside one of the rectangular Tuniit homes. He was piling the stones of its low walls back together, but doing so in a dazed, haphazard fashion. When Kannujaq saw his face, it was contorted with agony, glistening with tears. The eyes were wide. Fevered. As though gazing off at nothing in particular. As though the old man had gone mad. Kannujaq barely tore his gaze away from the old creature in time to avoid stepping over two women who were lying on top of a fallen man. Their long, despairing wails seemed to merge into a single voice.

The Glaring One's hulking men had killed without purpose, seemingly laying into whomever had made themselves most available. It was an angry, insane sort of thing, and even accounts Kannujaq had heard of revenge-based attacks between families had not seemed as awful as this. Where people had not been available, the brutes had attacked and scattered the cooking fires. They had even kicked in the feeble little walls that made up the Tuniit homes.

Kannujaq felt awkward as Tuniit grieved and pitifully restored order all around him. He began to stare downward, not wanting to take in any more of it. He passed only one person who seemed to notice that he was not a Tuniq: a young mother who clutched her baby tighter at the sight of him. But Siku led Kannujaq along even faster, quickly bringing him to his own little, Tuniit-style place: a sunken, square-walled hovel strewn with odd carvings, bones, and bags deformed with the overstuffing of nebulous materials. It was all, Kannujaq supposed, a shaman's garbage. But Kannujaq wasn't sure whether he was witnessing a shaman's lifestyle, or simply a boy's tendency to collect things.

On reflex, Kannujaq moved to the left side of the house—the polite thing to do among his own folk, though it might have meant nothing here. He spotted some dried meat, snatched it up and chewed, as was any guest's right. The boy ignored him, stuffing fistfuls of heather into a near-dead fire. This place was a miniature version of what Kannujaq guessed to be the typical Tuniit home. The flagstone floor was a shallow pit, given the illusion of greater height by the rectangle of short stone walls around it. The ceiling was tent-like. Kannujaq didn't have time to study it closely, since he was nearly overwhelmed by smoke billowing from the fire. He began to cough, but Siku just grinned at him from a cloud of fumes, seemingly unbothered.

Sooty Ones, Kannujaq thought, recalling his people's alternate name for the Tuniit. *No wonder!* This, at least, was exactly as he'd heard: It seemed that the Tuniit did not use *qulliit*—the seal-oil lamps, painstakingly carved from soapstone, that were so central to the homes of his own kind. But then again, women alone were the owners of qulliit, and this dwelling bore every indication that the boy lived by himself.

Where, Kannujaq wondered, *is this kid's family?*

Maybe the boy was an orphan. Or perhaps he lived in some shaman-related seclusion as part of Tuniit custom . . .

Kannujaq was so tired. It seemed almost painful to keep wondering about everything. To force his mind along, like urging his dog team. To keep thinking . . .

There was a weird smell that accompanied the smoke. Sharp, but not entirely unpleasant. Within a few heartbeats, Kannujaq's muscles relaxed, like so many dog tethers suddenly cut. He may not have felt much like thinking—but, odd as it seemed, he very much felt like talking.

"Really funny," slurred Kannujaq to the boy, "thinking I could help with those giant-men. As if anyone could. It's like you think I'm a Tuniq."

Kannujaq gave his head a shake. His voice sounded a bit strange to his own ears.

The boy grinned at him.

Oh, we forgot to tell you: Shamans were also pretty clever when it came to the things that plants and other natural materials could do. Kannujaq, as it turned out, was right. The boy was an angakkuq—a shaman—and the lad had drugged him with the smoke from his fire. There's no way to know exactly why he did such a thing. After all, we only know what Kannujaq was thinking, not the boy. But the young shaman probably wasn't trying to be mean. If we had to guess, we'd say that he just sensed how freaked out Kannujaq was, and wanted to force a chat with him. Maybe it wasn't the nicest thing to do, making Kannujaq breathe that smoke without telling him what it was. We don't know what it was, either, and we're telling this tale! Let's just hope the boy knew what he was doing, because breathing the smoke from anything is never a great idea.

5

Under a Gentle Tide

As it was, the winds rasped at the outside world, and the weeping of Tuniit gradually quieted down, and the hunter and the boy talked. For how long, Kannujaq was unsure—for it seemed that Siku had thrown something other than just heather onto the fire. And with every pinch of the dark, grey, crinkly stuff that burned, time washed away like sand under a gentle tide.

Nevertheless, Kannujaq quickly learned that this was not the first time the giant-men had attacked. There had been rumours that every Tuniit camp, near and far, had been assaulted. It was said that they wiped out whole communities, or at least tried to, always attacking men and women first. For whatever reason, they left children alone. Some Tuniit escaped them by fleeing inland. More died under their colossal, whirling knives. Always, the invaders laughed, shouting as they slaughtered, as though they were crazy people who thought that murder was like picking berries. And their shouts sounded like:

"Siaraili!"

The war cry of the raiders had become the

common name for them. And so it was that the giant-men were known to the Tuniit as *Siaraili*.

There had been peace over this last winter, during which time no Tuniq had heard anything of the Siaraili. But just last month, the monsters had again appeared at the shore, savagely assaulting this camp.

Ice is breaking up, Kannujaq thought, his mind clearing a bit as the stuff in the fire burned out. *Their loon-wolf-boat couldn't get here over wintertime.*

Kannujaq had heard that, unlike his own folk, the Tuniit rarely used boats. If that was true, it probably hadn't occurred to them that the giant-men—Siaraili or whatever they were called—depended on their vessel. It meant that they lived somewhere else, somewhere divided from the mainland by sea, and not in some other camp along the same coast as the Tuniit.

The shaman-boy had his own theories. Siku's belief, as it turned out, was that the Siaraili had followed Angula, this camp's current boss, to this part of the coast. And Siku claimed, with a scowl, that Angula was the cause of all this. Angula was a Tuniq who had brought himself into power, here, by lending tools to other camp people. Not just any tools. Special ones. Angula possessed a fabulous, secret hoard of "special" tools. And it was this collection, the boy claimed, that helped him buy his way into power everywhere he went.

Doesn't like Angula much, Kannujaq thought, watching the boy's features twist as he spoke of the man.

Kannujaq then learned why the boy had initially seemed so obsessed with his kannujaq necklace. According to Siku, every one of the special tools that Angula held so dear was made of the same stuff as Kannujaq's necklace. It was Siku's belief that Angula had somehow stolen these kannujaq things from the Glaring One himself. And now the giant-men, the Siaraili servants of the Glaring One, were searching for their master's missing goods.

With the difficulty in figuring out the boy's weird Tuniq way of talking, this much of the little shaman's account had taken some time to tell. The effects of the smoke had almost entirely passed, and Kannujaq's thoughts were becoming more focused, sharp as an arrow point. It occurred to him, suddenly, that he might not be getting an accurate version of events, and he found himself wishing for some elders to consult with. That was not very likely to happen, though. Even the Tuniit who had not run from Kannujaq had at least refused to look him in the eye. The boy was the "friendliest" person here.

Almost unconsciously, Kannujaq found his head turning in the direction of where he had left his dogs. The longer he stayed in this place, the more he felt trapped. Listening to the boy made him feel as though he were committing to something—and that, he could not do. It was becoming clear that, in the boy's imaginative thinking, the loop of kannujaq material was a kind of sign from the unseen world that Kannujaq himself possessed a power that only the Glaring One and his giant-men had owned up until now.

The idea was cute. Even tragic. Despite the lad's special status, he still had the childish tendency to believe that events were connected. Kannujaq found himself wishing that he could state things plainly—tell Siku that things just happened. Not all things were signs. Not everything had meaning.

Still, Kannujaq held his tongue. He understood that the boy was afraid. Desperate. The Siaraili were a horror beyond understanding. And Kannujaq's arrival was sheer accident.

How might two senseless things combine to make sense?

Kannujaq could only put up with so much of Siku's imagination. He was not about to stay.

The boy still held a bit of the crinkly, mystery stuff in his hand—the gunk that he threw on the fire along with the heather to produce smoke—and he leaned over to toss more of it into the flames. Kannujaq, almost grabbing him by the wrist, prevented him from doing so.

"No more smoke," he told the lad. "Just tell me. Is this Angula person still the camp's boss?"

The boy used his face to indicate "yes," raising eyebrows and widening his eyes. This startled Kannujaq: It was one of the facial expressions his own folk used to agree with something. Before Kannujaq could think about it further, though, Siku rushed into more complaints about Angula.

It seemed that Angula, the Tuniq boss whom Siku portrayed as such a villain, had become mad with the idea of power. Increasingly, Angula had begun to claim that spirits were giving him his kannujaq tools. He had even begun to claim that his tools gave him, and those who followed him, special powers.

Crazy, Kannujaq thought.

It was Siku's belief, apparently, that Angula wanted to think of himself as an angakkuq—a shaman. Maybe even something beyond a common shaman. These were strange times. With raids by the Siaraili, people were no longer sure what to believe. Some had given in to Angula's ideas. Many Tuniit simply wanted to leave, even despite their intense love of their homes. But in his madness and power lust, Angula would not let anyone go.

They love their homes? Kannujaq thought. He couldn't help smiling at the weird notion. This at least answered a question that had been lurking in the back of Kannujaq's mind: If the Tuniit were under attack from the sea, why did they not simply move away? To Kannujaq's folk, home was a dog team, a temporary shelter, or wherever he could meet up with relatives for a while.

Kannujaq kept listening, and Siku explained that Angula's latest bit of madness had been to tell the Tuniit community that the Siaraili were under his direction. Their attacks, the crazy man claimed, were punishment for the camp folk disobeying his orders. According to Angula, the Siaraili attacks would stop as soon as people dropped any idea of leaving, and demonstrated complete submission to Angula's will.

Kannujaq fidgeted as he listened. He was uneasy with this story about Angula, and wondered whether the boy was exaggerating. Among Kannujaq's people, it was a terrible thing to force one's will on another. In truth, if there was anything that Kannujaq's people could have called sacred, it might have been respect for the *isuma*—the personal feelings and thoughts of each individual.

Kannujaq had descended into a spiral of his own dark thoughts, so he was startled when Siku suddenly tossed something. The object landed with a heavy "clunk" on one of the home's flagstones. Kannujaq stared at it for a moment, amazed, before picking it up.

He immediately noted the weight of the object. It was obviously a kind of knife, but it was much heavier than it ought to have been. The knives that Kannujaq's people used were small, typically made of ivory, bone, or antler, and they were feather-light in comparison to this one. He blinked, examining the blade, and a sudden realization almost made him forget to breathe.

Tuniit, thought Kannujaq, *could never have made this thing!* Their craftsmanship was legendary for its poor quality. And, while Siku's clothes seemed to have been tailored well enough, the rest of these camp folk were dressed in what—to Kannujaq's family—might have been rags. The few tools Kannujaq had seen here were little better. No lamps. No dogsleds or the kit that went with them. No boats. Kannujaq wasn't sure how the Tuniit managed to survive at all.

But this knife was of excellent quality. And what most caught Kannujaq's attention, what even frightened him a bit, was the colour: the dark red of a kannujaq blade. It was cold, like stone. Like the loop that hung from his own necklace. Yet this was no little scrap, the remainder of what had once been a grandmother's needle. This blade was almost as long as Kannujaq's forearm, having only a single, straight edge. The dull side was oddly curved, and along it ran mysterious etchings.

Decoration?

Kannujaq scratched at it with his fingernail. Rust, as could be found on some rocks, came away from the blade. Under the rust was a grey stuff, hard and cold. It was very much like kannujaq, but more dense. Stone could leave scratches on his own sample of kannujaq. But when he took the strange tool and scraped it along one of the floor's flagstones, there was almost no scoring. Kannujaq clamped his teeth on the object, but he immediately sensed that it would shatter every tooth in his mouth before giving way.

His heart began to race.

6

The Great Angula

The boy had made a mistake. This knife was not made of kannujaq! The material was something like kannujaq, but far, far better. Kannujaq had assumed that, when Siku had spoken of "tools," the boy had meant little things, like needles or hooks or bits for hand-rotated drills. But this . . .

The hunter in Kannujaq began to think about what he could do with such material. He thought:

And the boy says Angula owns a lot of this stuff?

While Kannujaq turned the knife in wonder, already feeling a bit resentful that he had to give the tool back, Siku explained that it was one that Angula was lending him in return for various services. The hint of a mischievous smile, however, told Kannujaq that the boy had stolen it.

Then Kannujaq sat up. He stared into the boy's wide blue eyes. How could he begin to explain what danger the Tuniit were in? If the Glaring One was indeed angry at the loss of these objects, as Siku had claimed, and if the giant-men owned many more of these treasures . . .

Kannujaq never got the chance to speak. A voice, deep, as though from a chest more bear than man, suddenly boomed from outside.

"Why, I wonder?" the speaker bellowed. "Why does our baby shaman hide a dogsledder in our camp?"

Siku went rigid, and the look of him told Kannujaq that the strange voice belonged to Angula.

"I wonder," bellowed Angula again, "what a dogsledder wants from we Tuniit!"

Taking in a deep breath, then releasing it again as a sigh, Kannujaq stepped outside to face the voice's owner. There, he saw before him the fattest imaginable Tuniq man, chest adorned with set over set of clumsily arranged bear-tooth amulets. Rather than dangle, they seemed to rest on his middle-aged paunch. As a Tuniq, he was already rather short and squat. The added weight simply enhanced the boulder-like appearance that all Tuniit men possessed.

Here, Kannujaq thought, unimpressed, *is the great Angula.*

Angula stood flanked by three younger men, who watched Kannujaq out of the corners of their eyes, as though hoping he might vanish like some trick of the Land. Kannujaq—whose skepticism toward Siku's storytelling had waned on hearing, then seeing, Angula—suspected that the young men were Angula's cronies. Their allegiance had been bought with Angula's treasures. Fortunately, there were no weapons of any kind, much less those made of kannujaq, anywhere in sight. Kannujaq could see several other Tuniit men, women, and children, milling around behind Angula.

Everywhere Kannujaq looked, there were nervous glances.

Then, Kannujaq espied the first beautiful thing that he had seen since coming to the Tuniit camp.

It was a woman: one with eyes like dark stones

beneath sunlit water. But the lines of her face suggested that she did more frowning than smiling. Her hair was worn in normal braids, rather than in the crazy Tuniit way, and her clothes were of unusually high quality . . .

Wait! thought Kannujaq. *She's no Tuniq!*

She looked like one of his own people!

Though it took some effort, since she was lovely, Kannujaq forced his eyes from the woman. He greeted Angula perhaps a bit too late, for Angula ignored every sign of friendliness that Kannujaq tried to show, making only a bearlike chuffing noise in response. Again, Angula began to wonder—and loudly—why there was a "stranger hiding in his camp." While he did so, Angula's cronies snickered next to him. Their eyes, however, as with most of the Tuniit here, betrayed the fact that they were uncomfortable with Angula's rude behaviour.

Angula, it seemed, not only knew of Kannujaq's "dogsledder" folk, but obviously had a problem with them. He spoke as a show of dominance, it seemed, for the sake of the onlookers, rather than directly addressing Kannujaq. He drove home his remarks by turning to look Kannujaq up and down, from moment to moment, wrinkling his face in disgust.

"It is obvious," Angula went on, "that this is why the Siaraili have attacked yet again! This is a camp full of disobedience. I have been defied once more, for now someone has tried to hide one of the foreign dogsledders among us."

Then the bully spotted the kannujaq knife, still held in Kannujaq's hand.

"What is this?" he exploded, going eye-to-eye with some of the folk. They seemed to shrink back from him, intimidated by his rage.

"A dogsledder comes among us to steal!" he fumed. "It is bad enough that their dogsledding kind always soil our traditional lands! But now the trespassers steal from us!"

Kannujaq noted that Angula was fond of that term: "dogsledder." The bully used it a bit too much for Kannujaq's liking. The word seemed to convey some particular, special brand of hatred that Angula bore toward Kannujaq's folk; and something hot in Kannujaq's insides began to curl and hiss. Rather than speak out of fury, saying something he might later regret, Kannujaq stood rigid, keeping his lips pressed together.

Then Angula wheeled and pointed at Kannujaq, for the first time addressing him directly:

"You are jealous! That's why you have come to steal! You dogsledding foreigners always think you have better things than Tuniit! But now a Tuniq has better things than you. And you can't live with it, can you?"

Kannujaq remained shocked into silence throughout the tirade. But Angula's shameful antics were not allowed to continue. A youthful voice suddenly barked from Kannujaq's rear:

"Angula!"

Siku had emerged from his home. His blue eyes had paled further with rage, becoming like white sparks burning in Angula's direction. While all the camp stood silent, the boy uncurled the fingers of one palm.

Siku revealed his helper.

Shamans could have many helpers. These could be the monstrous and unseen beings they had ritually bound under their willpower, or the willing souls of animals or ancestors. Everything under the Sky had the potential for life. And so a helper could be dog or a piece of seaweed; a giant or a bumblebee; one's grandmother or a stone. Often, a helper was simply too bizarre for description. Helpers had only one thing in common: like the shaman, they were filled with the Strength of the Land. Helpers were not spiritual, in that they were neither worshipped nor held to be sacred. But their powers could be useful.

Kannujaq got one brief glimpse at a tiny, skeletal figure in the boy's palm—a carved figurine that symbolized the helper—before he turned his gaze away. Among Kannujaq's folk, it could be unhealthy to stare too long at some-seen things from the world of shamans. Maybe it was the same with the Tuniit.

Kannujaq heard gasps from the crowd all around him.

Then the boy began to speak at Angula. His voice was spidery. High-pitched. Nothing like that of the lad who had just spent the last little while telling Kannujaq about Angula and the Siaraili raids.

Kannujaq quickly realized that it was the helper, who announced itself as That One Bearing, speaking through the boy. No one would ever see That One Bearing (unless they were another helper or a shaman). But the boy could symbolize the helper through the figurine that he himself, or another shaman who had taught him, had carved. The figurine was just a representation, but for the moment, no less "real" than the helper itself. If necessary, Siku could also arm That One Bearing with invisible weapons, similar carvings of tiny knives or spears. Then he might send the helper to stab at somebody's soul, making them sick.

Kannujaq hoped, however, that Siku was not that kind of angakkuq.

It seemed, for now, that the helper was here as no more than a messenger. Borrowing Siku's voice to do its speaking, That One Bearing told Angula:

"You are no longer boss of this camp. It is the dogsledder who must become the camp's leader for a time. It is the kannujaq he wears about his neck, a thing the Siaraili also bear, that is a sign of this fact. It is up to the dogsledder to drive away the Siaraili."

Drive the Siaraili away? thought Kannujaq. *No way! I don't even want to be here!*

Then the helper addressed the other Tuniit, saying:

"Angula's sins have brought the Siaraili among you. You will all perish if you continue to have Angula as leader. This I know by Hidden knowledge. If you doubt me, simply look at the dogsledder's necklace to see that his folk have power to match that of Siaraili."

I don't! Kannujaq thought. *I don't! Why would the helper say such an untrue thing?*

Kannujaq began to wonder if it was the helper, or Siku himself, doing the talking here.

One way or another, the helper did not finish the message. There was a roar, and Angula rushed forward, knocking the shaman boy down.

All onlookers, including Kannujaq, stood paralyzed with shock. It was not that Angula had attacked a shaman. It was not even that he had attacked a boy. It was that he had done it openly. In front of everyone. Open violence, above all violence, was no different from madness. At least, that was the case among Kannujaq's people . . . .

Crazy, thought Kannujaq, staring at Angula, who stood wide-eyed, panting like an animal.

Angula's out of his mind.

The mysterious, beautiful, non-Tuniit woman was by Siku's side in an instant, though the young shaman was back up on his feet after only a moment. His blue eyes were fixed on Angula. Kannujaq had never before seen such murder in a young boy's gaze.

Angula was still panting, perhaps more with stress than exertion, and he quickly whirled about, pointing at Kannujaq.

"This is exactly what I was afraid of!" he bellowed. "Look what you made me do! You are an evil angakkuq, manipulating us all!"

But his eyes shifted about, a bit frightened and uncertain.

"I will forgive Siku!" Angula huffed. "He is just under your dogsledder control! But you will leave now! Try to stay, and you die!"

Angula glanced at his cronies, but they looked scared, uneasy with the situation. They refused to gaze directly at Kannujaq.

"None of us," Angula roared at the Tuniit, "is to follow this dogsledder! Or listen to his lies! Anyone who does so will die!"

For a time, the only motion in the world seemed to be windcast snow. The only sounds were those howls and yips of Kannujaq's distant dog team, anxious for his return. Kannujaq began to ache for his dogs. He had never so wanted to leave this horrid place.

After a long moment, Kannujaq threw down Angula's knife at his feet. He then stepped over the kannujaq blade, and walked away. His dark eyes briefly met Siku's blue ones. The boy seemed confused. Maybe he felt a bit betrayed. For a moment, Kannujaq almost paused, almost opened his mouth to apologize to the young shaman.

But why should he? He hadn't done anything wrong. He had made no promises of assistance to the Tuniit. He was only here, among them, because he and his dogs had mistaken the place for a human camp. Well . . . maybe the Tuniit were also human. In a way. But that didn't mean Kannujaq owed them anything.

They're Tuniit, and they're crazy, he thought as he shouldered his way past the sooty camp folk. *And I'm not a bad person for leaving them.*

I'm not.

7

Angula's Treasure

While you were reading, we were just discussing whether or not Kannujaq had done the right thing. Leaving the Tuniit to their fate, that is. After all, from what Kannujaq had seen of the Siaraili, they were pretty intimidating. He was wrong about the Tuniit being crazy—they were just scared and had their own ways of understanding things, and that can make people seem a bit nuts, sometimes. But what Kannujaq really needed to understand was that he was part of a larger world, and his people could no longer keep roaming without expecting to bump into other weird folk. In the end, life would not leave him any choice: the wider Arctic was a fact that he had to face. Keep reading and you'll see what we mean.

Kannujaq went straight to his dogs. There were sounds behind him as he left: Angula roaring at people, making more announcements. He ignored it all and left the sounds of the Tuniit foolishness behind him.

And there were his dogs. He had never realized,

until that moment, how much he loved these shaggy, jumping, yipping creatures. He had never realized what a treasure he possessed in his simple sled.

Kannujaq only had scraps of dried meat to throw for the dogs, but it would keep them going. The storm had pretty much passed, leaving a bit of snow behind. It was an ideal time for departure. He went to see if everything was lashed down properly in the sled. Then he went to relieve himself.

He took a step. There was the sudden flutter of wings. White appeared out of nowhere—a male ptarmigan hidden in an old snow patch. The potential food item nearly flew straight over his head, and Kannujaq desperately looked around for a rock to wing it with.

Then he saw them.

There were four of them, one grossly fat. Kannujaq knew that that one was Angula. So, he had decided not to let Kannujaq live, after all. They were coming on fast, carrying obscenely long knives, all made of the stuff that Siku had believed to be kannujaq—and much larger than the knife the boy had shown him.

Angula, Kannujaq realized, had taken out his treasures.

They also carried bows and arrows in hand. This was not about fighting. It was about murder. They would cripple him with arrows. Finish him with blades.

Kannujaq raced to the sled and frantically pulled away the lashings, retrieving his own bow. His heart seemed to thunder in his ears by the time he found arrows and stepped away from the dogs. He wanted no stray shots falling among them.

The Tuniit apparently noticed his actions. They froze. He could see the cronies darting questioning looks at Angula. Their mouths were moving. Kannujaq could see the puffs of their breath in the cold air.

Probably trying to convince Angula that this is a bad idea, he thought.

It was.

Angula ignored his cronies. He nocked an arrow and drew, aiming high for a good arc.

Kannujaq backed up and the arrow fell short. And Kannujaq finally released the breath that he had held, due to mingled fright and anxiety, in his chest. As a wanderer, a hunter, his life depended on alertness. Paying attention to details. Back in the Tuniit camp, he had noted the ways in which Tuniit tended to construct things. To lash and tie objects together. He had been unimpressed with their craftsmanship. He had suspected—hoped—that their bows could not send an arrow very far. Fortunately, he now saw that he'd been right.

Angula tried again. This time, his cronies joined in. Several arrows came at Kannujaq, but he again backed up, and they fell short. This happened twice more, and with every failed attack, Kannujaq's smile grew broader.

Kannujaq smiled because he did not bear anything like a Tuniit bow. His was made according to the standards of his own folk, from carefully carved segments of whalebone, lashed together in a style that made it strong and reliable.

Its range was greater.

Kannujaq carefully nocked his arrow. He took his time in drawing back the string. His breath was held once again—but now with concentration rather than anxiety. He made sure of his stance.

And shot.

The arrow was almost beautiful, like a bird as it arced through the air.

It came down, burying itself in Angula's chest. There, the arrow quivered, before Angula fell to one knee. His cry was long. More a wail of despair than of pain. He fell like some boulder that had rolled over shifting ground.

And lay still.

Kannujaq was nocking another arrow when the cronies at last tore their eyes from Angula's body. Not having really wanted a fight in the first place, they fled like startled hares.

Kannujaq issued long expletives under his breath. He hated this.

He walked over to the fallen Angula, frowning, somehow far more angry at Angula's corpse than he had been at the living man.

Idiot! he thought. *Madman! Making me kill him. The less-than-nothing fool has made me into a murderer.*

Kannujaq suddenly felt dirty. As though he were now something less than human. As though he should go into hiding.

Though his arrows were precious, Kannujaq made no attempt to retrieve the one that still quivered, its fletching stirred by wind, in Angula's chest. He stood watching its movements for a time, sickened and confused by the feelings this encounter had left him with. Here was the one thing he could not stand: human smallness. The Land, despite its dangers, had never frustrated him. The Land had never lied, or grasped, or pretended to be anything other than what it was. It was only the narrow-minded behaviour of humanity that could leave Kannujaq feeling this way—hollow and weak.

This, the killing of Angula, had not been necessary. And the greed, the ego, the stupidity of it all brought Kannujaq to a kind of certainty:

The Tuniit are human, he thought. *They are.*

He put his bow away and began to leave. But then he paused.

He actually found himself concerned about the Tuniit. How would things unfold once the Siaraili returned? Maybe better, with Angula gone. But now they had no one to lead them. Would they have the wits to flee? Or would they sit, confused, waiting to be slaughtered? And where would they go? As long as they lived by a coast, that Siaraili loon-wolf-boat might hunt them down.

It might even find Kannujaq's own folk.

Wherever his family now camped, it was sure to be along some coast or other. Would they not look up one day, startled by the sight of a great loon, having no idea that it brought madness and murder?

He looked back toward the Tuniit camp, now leaderless. He remembered the ptarmigan. It was his friend-animal. If it had not taken flight, Angula and the cronies would have ambushed him. Could it be a sign that he really was supposed to work against the enemies of the Tuniit?

"No," he grumbled to himself. "Probably means I'll get killed along with them."

He shook his head, once again swearing in the drawn-out, colourful way of his people. He swore mostly at himself, for beginning to think in terms of signs. Like Siku.

Siku—he was a shaman, but he was also a boy. Would he be able to hold the Tuniit camp together?

Well, there was no point in sledding away so quickly. He might as well tell Siku what had happened. Siku, young as he was, was somewhat respected. He might point the Tuniit to a new leader.

As long as it wasn't Kannujaq.

He gave the dogs the rest of his dried meat, then walked back to the Tuniit camp.

8

Under the Flagstone

Siku was overjoyed at Kannujaq's return. The lad even puffed himself up, striding about as though he had doubled in height, as though he had predicted every detail of what had occurred. In his weird shaman's way, the boy saw Angula's death as assurance of exactly what Kannujaq refused to accept: that he was here to save the Tuniit.

At least Angula's hold on the community, one based solely on terror, had been eroded. Some individuals actually smiled, however shyly, at Kannujaq. Enough people offered him food that he had to start refusing it.

One of the first things Siku did was to introduce him to his mother, Siaq. She greeted Kannujaq with coolness. This was the lovely woman whom Kannujaq had earlier spotted. Kannujaq was still pretty sure, given her clothing style and overall bearing, that she was not Tuniit in origin—probably one of his own folk. But what was she doing here?

There was no chance to ask. Siku had something of great importance to show him.

In the Tuniit community, only two other people had lived in the same secrecy and solitude as the boy shaman. One was Siaq, Siku's mother. The other was Angula. Siaq had served Angula over the years. She was not his wife, though Angula had taken many wives, never keeping any. No, Siku's mother had only ever been one thing to Angula: his slave.

Angula's empty home was left untouched, as though it were now a haunted place. So there was no one there to greet them as Siku led Kannujaq into it. It was large. Not as big as some Tuniit dwellings, since Tuniit liked to group many families together in a single place, but it was large enough for a family of a decent size. There was something grave-like about it, Kannujaq thought, now that it was abandoned.

It's the fire, Kannujaq realized, his eyes finding the spot in the floor where Tuniit traditionally burned their handfuls of heather. There was nothing burning there at the moment. *It's like Angula, now. Dead.*

Siku did not pause for a heartbeat. With his typical feverish intensity, he led Kannujaq to the rear of the place, where there was a kind of adjoining chamber meant for storage. There was little of value in here. Just some old, ragged caribou hides. But Kannujaq had already developed a suspicion concerning what he was about to see.

Sure enough, Siku pulled away all the trash to reveal overly large flagstones. There was one in particular on which Siku set his attention. The boy hooked fingers onto the edge of it, heaving in grunts and spasms. With each heave, he shifted the stone about the width of a little fingernail.

Kannujaq got tired of watching, waiting, so he knelt with Siku to help move the stone.

The weight of the thing! Kannujaq was embarrassed to let the boy see him straining. It was amazing to think that the timid Tuniit moved such stones around all the time. He reminded himself that Siku's mother was not a Tuniq—so neither was the boy a Tuniq, even though he had grown up among them.

Kannujaq had never before thought of himself as weak. But alongside the boy, he found himself smiling grimly, thinking:

We're almost unable to move this thing, even working together. How long must the kid have taken, doing it himself? Then putting it back again!

But Kannujaq's folk were all about working together to do things. Once he coaxed Siku into heaving to a certain rhythm, pulling at the same time as Kannujaq, the flagstone quickly slid aside.

Here were Angula's treasures.

Kannujaq realized that he was looking at all the things the Glaring One so desperately wanted back. All the things that Angula had stolen. Given what he already knew of the blade Siku had first shown him, then those even more monstrous blades hefted by Angula and his cronies at the time of Angula's killing, Kannujaq had developed the idea that few other objects could impress him.

So wrong—he'd been so wrong!

The pit was crammed with treasure.

Not one item in this pit, not one, was as poor as Siku's rusted knife. There were knives here, yes, but of such fine quality as to render Siku's laughable. And there was little in the trove that showed rust. As Kannujaq went through the pile—gingerly at first, then with increasing enthusiasm—he found blades like those that Angula and his cronies had carried, but better. It was clear that Angula had not allowed anyone to openly view his real treasure.

Parts of these Siaraili blades gleamed like captured sunlight. They were actually beautiful, as though their makers had wanted them to please the eye. Kannujaq nodded as he inspected the work. His own people were the same as the Siaraili in this way, wanting tools to be well made, but also splendid to look at. But . . . the sheer artistry of these treasures, combined with their hugeness, soon raised some doubt in Kannujaq's mind as to whether they had ever been intended as workaday tools. Some were so polished that he could see his own face reflected in their surfaces, as though he were regarding his image in wind-stirred water. The most polished blade in the pit was as long as Kannujaq's arm, shining like a fish belly, handle decorated with some sun-coloured substance. Its home was a sheath made of fine leather, wood, and what looked to be wolf fur.

This was pretty, but Kannujaq was more impressed with the tools that suggested working practicality. The majority were heavy, curving crescents—a bit like a woman's *ulu*. Among Kannujaq's people, an ulu was a common personal tool, usually made by a husband for his wife. But it was small! These Siaraili tools were over a hand span in size, attached to the sturdiest wooden hafts that Kannujaq had ever hefted.

With this stuff, he kept thinking, *you could hack through anything.*

And he shuddered, suddenly, remembering the Tuniit victims. He remembered what Siku had told him of how the Siaraili loved to kill.

Mad as it seemed, Kannujaq wondered:

Are these meant for people?

He shuddered again.

Then he remembered more of Siku's words. The Siaraili, bloodthirsty as they were, never harmed children. But why did they so hate men and women?

There were other things, as well. Spearheads. Arrowheads. Not a single object made of flint, jade, or ivory. Everything was of enormous size. It took Kannujaq some time to figure out that some items were belts. Other things he recognized as the strange bowls worn on the heads of the giant-men. Were they for protection? In case the Siaraili used such fierce weapons on each other? There was also a silvery, flexible thing, shaped like a coat; but made of tiny, tiny rings. There were curved plates with no apparent function. Maybe for serving food? And there were necklaces. Rings. All were made of different stones set in shining kannujaq-like stuff, gleaming as though they contained coloured fires.

"We must keep no part of this," Siku told him, eyeing Kannujaq's fingers as they brushed across an arrowhead.

Kannujaq grunted, unsure of what to say. Unsure of what he felt.

9

A Heavier Truth

By the time Kannujaq had pawed through it all, he was breathless. At the same time, he was a bit sad. Here was even more evidence that Angula had been mad. A sane man would have used such objects as tools, not weapons. As well, he would have shared them with friends and family. Life on the Land was hard enough, at times, without greed and stupidity to worsen it.

Mostly, Kannujaq felt panic. He now understood why the Glaring One wanted to regain these treasures. How, in all imagining, had Angula managed to steal this stuff?

Together, Kannujaq and Siku replaced the items. Then Siku took Kannujaq back to his grubby little shaman's house. The boy's mother, Siaq, was there. She looked up, giving Kannujaq an icy stare as he entered. As Kannujaq found a place to sit, the young shaman suddenly slipped back outside, leaving the man and woman alone.

Planned meeting, Kannujaq thought.

For a long moment, there was silence. Finally, when Kannujaq could stand it no more, he asked Siaq why she lived among Tuniit. Especially as a slave.

Siku's mother sighed, as though having dreaded the possibility of discussing such things. Then she placed something small and dark in the fire. There was thick smoke, but not that of heather. There came to Kannujaq's nostrils a sharp and familiar smell, but not as strong as when the boy had tended the fire. Within a few heartbeats, his wild spirals of thought and anxiety gave way to relaxation. Even a bit of stupidity. He glared at the woman, fighting the smoke's effects.

"Throw no more of that on the fire," he told her. When she stared back at him defiantly, he added, "If you do, I'm leaving. Only I control my isuma. You're not a Tuniq. You should know that."

Siaq issued a light hiss at him, her dark eyes narrowing in displeasure. But she tucked away a bag from which she had pulled the smelly angakkuq stuff. This was not a nice way to start a conversation, but Kannujaq had at least learned an important fact about her.

She, too, he thought to himself, *is an angakkuq*.

More silence. The fire burned. Kannujaq coughed. The smoke cleared. And so did his mind.

Just as Kannujaq was becoming convinced that this meeting was a waste of time, Siaq spoke.

"I had a husband once," she muttered.

She spoke in the manner of Kannujaq's folk. He was surprised to feel such relief at hearing the sound.

"But a time came," Siaq continued, "when he did not come home. I was alone, and I began to starve, eating my clothing in order to survive."

Kannujaq swallowed hard. The Land was indeed unkind, at times. Since all clothes were simply the skins of animals, they could be eaten. But it was a rare horror when someone was desperate enough to do so.

"In this state," said the woman, "I was found by the Tuniit. Even then, they were led by Angula. He was

less brutal in those days. Less mad. But not by much. He took me in as a slave, since I could do waterproof stitching. The Tuniit cannot. The Tuniit do not like slaves, but Angula always had his way through bullying. And a slave's life among Tuniit is better than death."

Hardly, Kannujaq thought to himself. But he did not speak. He knew that one must never interrupt a story. To do so was to insult a storyteller's isuma. He decided to interrupt Siaq only if she tried to throw more stuff on the fire.

"Angula attracts strange beings," Siaq added with a sigh. "One spring, the Tuniit discovered a great boat, wood instead of skin, lying gutted along the shore. There were beast-men there, Siaraili, covered in furs and hard shells. Their faces were like dog hair. Their bodies had gotten wet. They lay frozen, dead, stuck to the ground. Only one among them had not quite died."

In the absence of the weird smoke, Kannujaq's mind was fully clear. He instantly guessed which Siaraili had been rescued by the Tuniit.

Glaring One? he wondered.

"Angula dragged him to camp," Siaq said. "I was made to care for him. He was huge, like a giant. His hair was disgusting. Like a dog's. Skin disgusting, like a corpse's. He recovered quickly."

Siaq, her own face rather corpse-like in its smoke-framed slackness, turned toward her pile of kindling. Kannujaq readied himself to speak out, for he could not stand any more of the dark shaman-stuff. But Siaq reached only for dried heather. The white smoke of the heather, stifling as it was in tight quarters, seemed like a breath of fresh air in comparison to what she had earlier burned.

"This one," she went on, "this survivor . . . this was the one who you call the Glaring One. The one who hates us now. But, back then, he was only grateful to Angula. He repaid Angula by intimidating others in the camp for him. Angula enjoyed it. It was like having a bear as a pet. In time, Angula made me teach the Glaring One some of the way Tuniit speak. More than anything else, Angula's pet wanted to get home, which he said was across the sea. What he could not know was that great boats were spotted now and again, probably searching for him. Cunning Angula always found ways to keep the Glaring One out of sight of these boats, unaware of their presence. He kept him distracted with hunting. With games. With . . . many things."

Kannujaq shifted in discomfort.

"Always," Siku's mother continued, "I was there for whatever the Glaring One needed. Angula gave me over like a dog pup. The Glaring One was happy to have a slave, I think. Slaves were common where he came from—a place he called *Gronland.* His kind called the worthless Tuniit lands *Heluland*, or 'Place of Flat Stones.'"

Siaq broke off to wipe at her eyes, which were tearing. Her story died for a time. Kannujaq remained respectfully silent, watching the fire diminish to a low, ashy glow.

"But I was laughing at him, inside, all the time," the woman said a while later, as though there had been no pause in her tale, "because I knew that the Glaring One was just Angula's slave, like me. He just didn't know it."

She paused, reaching out a lean hand to push at some leftover twigs, stirring the fire around.

"Seasons went by," said the woman, "and I became sickened with it all. I started to tease Angula. I told him, sometimes, that I would tell the Glaring One how Angula was keeping him from being rescued. Angula beat me terribly for this, threatened to kill me. He was scared. He was not only keeping the Glaring One captive, but he had also searched the bodies of the Glaring One's dead companions. He had taken as much treasure as he could find. Knives. Spears. Arrows. Even some of the things they wore. He had told the Glaring One that they and their kannujaq implements had been lost to the sea."

She smiled darkly at Kannujaq, who shuddered at her words. Among his own folk, only a monster would think of stripping the dead. It was as bad as disturbing a grave.

"But he had actually kept the kannujaq tools," she added, "hiding them safely away. In time, the Glaring One grew into the Tuniit community. He even began to treat me kindly. But I was always tempted to tell him the truth about Angula. Then a night came when the Glaring One and I were quarrelling. All of my hate came out, somehow, made my mouth move on its own. I told him the truth. I told him everything. Every bit of it. Almost."

Siaq paused to throw a generous handful of heather onto the near-dead coals. After a moment, it crackled, and orange flame flared high.

"He never spoke after that," she went on. "He never looked at me. Not at Angula. Not at the Tuniit."

Staring into the fire, her face yellowed by its glow, Siaq laughed.

"Angula became scared," she said. "But he was relieved when the Glaring One slipped away one day. No one saw him go. Maybe he sighted one of the ships of his folk. It wasn't long before Angula started showing a few of his kannujaq treasures around, claiming that spirits had given them to him, that he had special powers. He had learned that wealth can purchase souls. He began to lend his treasures out, in return for loyalty. In this way, he enslaved everyone."

Siaq released a strange sound, at once mournful and amused.

"Do you understand this lesson?" she asked

Kannujaq. "Wealth makes power. Power makes fear. Fear makes slaves."

Kannujaq's eyes were fixed, staring, on her half-mad face, peering like a shadowed mask through the heather's smoke.

"But Angula had made a mistake," Siaq told him, "for the Glaring One was no normal man. He was a leader among his own folk. Angula had only a few years to enjoy his power, before the Glaring One returned. And he brought Siaraili. He sent out his giant-like men to punish the Tuniit shore encampments, laughing, killing, always searching for Angula and his stolen . . . things. Others died, but Angula escaped every time. Angula became mad, paranoid, trying to hold onto his power. He claimed that the sea raiders were punishing the community for disobeying him. In time, every Tuniq in that camp was gone, killed or scattered. Angula survived, fleeing to a new Tuniit community—this one. Myself and Siku, who was smaller then, came with him. Here, over the next few years, it was easy for Angula to buy himself authority with his stolen garbage. And the whole thing started again."

Siaq was weeping openly by the time she was finished her tale—from what, exactly, Kannujaq could not tell. But there did seem to be plenty to weep about. Suddenly, he understood how little her son, Siku, truly knew of his mother. She had told the boy bits and pieces of truth, but he had interpreted everything through the eye of a shaman (as well as that of a young boy). To Siku, as with the other Tuniit here, this was a battle against sea-monsters. The Siaraili were bad tuurngait—shape-shifting creatures of the Land's unseen parts, influenced by things like personal thought and feeling. Siku's grasp of matters was weighed down with the signs and forces he believed to whirl all around him.

His mother's burden, in truth, was much heavier.

10

Weakling!

Only Siaq and Angula had known who the Siaraili really were: an entirely other folk, unlike either Tuniit or Kannujaq's people. Huge. Well-armed. Brutal.

Kannujaq returned truth with truth.

"If we don't leave this place," he said, "all of us . . . we'll die."

Siaq sniffed and agreed.

"I can't leave the Tuniit, though," she said. "I've been with them too long. They are friends, family. Life has more meaning among them, now, than it does among your—I mean, our kind."

She's become a Tuniq, Kannujaq thought.

"And the Tuniit are not like our folk," she said, "always travelling, always sledding. The Tuniit worship their homes. Their homes are part of them."

Kannujaq could not understand why anyone would be attached to a fixed home, but he told Siku's mother:

"No time for this, Siaq. No time. The Siaraili left only because they were worried about the storm. But once they feel safe again, they'll finish this camp. If the Tuniit will not move, because of love of their homes, then there is only one other thing they can do. They must return the stolen kannujaq goods. Leave them by the shore, and hope the Glaring One finds them—"

He was surprised to find Siaq laughing before he could complete his argument. Hers was a dry, bitter sort of laughter.

"I told you of how I taught the Glaring One our language," she said. "But I learned some of the Glaring One's language, too."

Siaq pointed to Kannujaq's necklace.

"That stuff," she told him, "they call 'copper.' It's the weakest of their materials. For their weapons, they use a different word. I can't remember it anymore."

She looked Kannujaq in the eye, offering a bitter smile.

"Have you ever wondered," she asked him, "about what the Tuniit call the giant-men?"

Kannujaq made no answer, though the dark look in Siaq's eyes raised the hairs on his neck. With each breath, each utterance, the woman seemed to abandon some further shred of her sanity.

"Your son told me," Kannujaq answered. "He said they shout a word when they attack. Siaraili! It's why the Tuniit call them Siaraili."

Siaq laughed. "The Tuniit," she said, "have no idea what this word means. Shall I tell you? The Glaring One's men are shouting, 'Skraeling!' In truth, they are calling to the Tuniit. Mocking them by summoning them to their deaths. Because they know that the Tuniit do nothing but panic when they are attacked. They run, and run some more. That is why they are called Skraeling. The word, in the language of the Glaring One's folk, means 'Weakling.' The Glaring One's people have spent many generations at war. They have grown fond of it.

This is why the giant-men run through the camp like children at play. Kicking walls in. Slashing at every man or woman in reach. Raiding is fun for them, and they have no respect for those who will not fight back. Like the Tuniit. After every raid, they gorge themselves on whatever they find in camp. They wash it down with the harsh tea-like stuff that they are fond of. The tea that makes them sleepy. And bloodthirsty again. Do you think such a people are here only for stolen tools? They want blood. They are mad!"

Kannujaq frowned, trying to make sense of the information.

"But," he argued, "they don't attack children. So they're not entirely—"

"You don't understand, do you?" hissed Siaq. "They are friends to violence! They don't like this Land, do you not see? They hate us, Tuniq or not, because we are part of it. Because they want to go home, and every stone of this place reminds them that they cannot. Their leader, the Glaring One, will not allow it until he has what is his!"

Kannujaq was confused. "Then let's give him the treasure," he said. "What else could he want?"

A strange look flashed through Siaq's features, but Kannujaq had no idea what it meant.

Kannujaq sighed. "Siaq," he said, trying to be patient, "your son thinks I'm here to fight off the Glaring One and his people. He thinks I'll rescue the Tuniit." He reached for his necklace, giving it a shake, so that his pitiful little loop of kannujaq gleamed in the firelight. "He thinks," Kannujaq added, "that this piece on my necklace, given to me by my grandparents, means I have some kind of power in common with the Glaring One."

Once again, Siaq laughed, and the response irritated Kannujaq. "Siku believes what I want him to," she said. "He knows what I permit, and he makes up the rest, like always."

"Then tell him the truth," pressed Kannujaq. "Tell him I have no special destiny here. Our futures are what we make of them. Maybe the Tuniit believe in destiny, but you are not a Tuniq! You are one of my kind. You must understand what I'm saying. We don't have to die. We can return the stolen property. Leave it on the beach for when the Glaring One next arrives. Flee and never speak of him again . . . ."

"Nothing will stop the Glaring One," muttered Siaq. Her arms were now folded around herself. She rocked, staring into the dying fire, and seemed almost to forget that Kannujaq was present. "Nothing," she added, "will make him quit."

Kannujaq sighed, rubbing at his sooty eyes. Maybe Siaq was right. He recalled the raid's end that he had witnessed. Such bloodshed. Such unnecessary murder. Perhaps the Glaring One wanted his property returned; but the way of his men was hardly that of a group in search of something. Unless that something were madness.

But these were barely men, were they? These were folk whose ship prow was carved to resemble a beast—a wolf. And that was how they attacked. The Tuniit were like mindless caribou, panicked and chased and inevitably slaughtered. They were all the victims. The caribou.

And the Siaraili were wolves.

Wolves, Kannujaq thought.

The notion repeated itself over and over in his mind.

Siaq was stuffing more heather into the fire, when Kannujaq asked her:

"How does a Tuniq hunt a wolf?"

"They don't," she said. "Wolf pelts, among the Tuniit, are rare and valuable. Because it is almost impossible to get near enough to a wolf to kill it."

But Kannujaq knew how his own folk hunted them.

One did not catch a wolf by running it down. Nor by ambushing it. The creatures were too wily. They could sense humans, evading them every time. Instead, one used a wolf's habits against it. A wolf was like a dog. If it found food lying about, it would stuff itself with as much as its gut could carry, eating faster than it could think. So Kannujaq's folk used this observation to their advantage: They crafted a trap that was frozen into a large chunk of fat or meat. The wolf gobbled it down without thought. When the food thawed in the wolf's stomach, the trap sprang.

Dead wolf.

Siku walked in while Kannujaq was trying to explain this idea to a disinterested Siaq. The boy shaman, however, immediately bent an ear to Kannujaq's words. He even seemed to grasp what Kannujaq was implying, and began to rummage through his bags. In a few moments, the lad had retrieved a handful of dried, hideous, near-black lumps. He held them out to Kannujaq, smiling, his blue eyes dancing in the firelight.

"Is that," Kannujaq asked, "what you burn to make people sleepy?"

Sick, too, he thought.

"It has a few uses," Siaq said without emotion, "depending on how it is prepared. It can make people dreamy, wanting to talk and tell the truth about things. But it can also make one very sick. It is rare, and very dangerous. It can make one forever stupid—even kill, if used by one who is already stupid. But an angakkuq, like myself or Siku, can prepare small amounts of it properly."

After a long moment, Kannujaq asked Siaq and her son, "You said it can kill?"

"If we made a thick soup of it," said the boy,

grinning his toothy grin.

Siaq frowned, her dark eyes growing wide. She glared at her son.

"Why would you do such a thing?" she asked him. "You know that you should never consume that stuff. It was one of the first lessons I taught you."

"It's not for any of us," said Kannujaq with a sigh. He hated this. This moment meant committing himself to a terrible act.

"Would it still work," he asked, "if we soaked some meat in it?"

"Yes," said Siku, sounding surprisingly mature in the firmness of his answer, "if we use enough. But I have three bags here."

Siaq, suddenly understanding, ran off to retrieve her own supplies.

Unhappy Kannujaq! Once again, when he'd only wanted peace, a life of exploring the wide Land, the violence of others pulled him into violent response. But, as his own elders might have reminded him, the Land is far more than rocks and lichen and hills and coasts. The Land is also those living beings, humanity being no exception, that dwell on its surface. Peace is possible only if all possess the will for it. And Kannujaq, without even knowing that he was doing so, had shifted his role from hunter to warrior.

It took a little over a day to ready everything, and the Tuniit needed a great deal of convincing. Kannujaq was aggressive about securing their promise that they would help out, when the moment arrived. Everyone's movements were planned. Rehearsed. The homes nearest the beach were left abandoned. Storage areas left full of meat. As many Tuniit as possible would share homes nearest the hills, allowing them a head start if the raiders were sighted. They were not to move far, but only to take cover near the base of the hills.

Kannujaq alone would creep back to the camp to see if the Glaring One's men took the bait. If so, he would signal.

There was no alternate plan.

11

Eyes of the Glaring One

The days were long now, so it was late evening when the Glaring One returned in creeping dusk.

One by one, the great boat's torches sprang to life as it reached the shore, to the roars of:

"Skraeling!"

"Skraeling!"

"Skraeling!"

The Tuniit camp, and especially Kannujaq himself, had already spent hours in nervous anticipation. All eyes were on the sea. Everything was set, and cries of alarm spread faster than flame in heather among the Tuniit, who were soon running inland with all the fleetness their stocky bodies could muster. Kannujaq ran alongside of them, desperate and hoping that the Tuniit would be able to summon their courage when the time came.

Kannujaq's great worry was that the raiders would not behave as expected. Siku and Siaq had prepared a kind of rancid-smelling tea out of their dried shaman stuff. Each had assured Kannujaq that the soup would be undetectable on meat that had soaked in it. They were wrong. Kannujaq himself had sampled the tiniest bit of the food. It had no peculiar scent, but its flavour was off. Bitter. Even from the nibble he had tried, his stomach had begun to lurch soon after swallowing. He had puked it all up before learning what else it had in store for him.

Maybe, he hoped, *the raiders will arrive hungry. Either that, or they're just stupid.*

The Tuniit reached the hills and many sheltering boulders, keeping low. Kannujaq could already spot commotion down by the beach. This turned out to be raiders kicking in the short walls and ripping the tops off of Tuniit homes. Stamping their way through cooking fires. Kannujaq gave them time, letting the rosy light of evening approach. After the amount of time it might have taken for someone to boil up soup, he began to creep back down, doing his best stalk, hoping that his now sooty clothes would help him blend in with the landscape.

It was like torture, creeping down to the beach, wondering with every beat of his heart if raider eyes were already tracking him. At last, he arrived at the edge of the community. Fortunately, there were many large rocks about the place—enough, at least, for him to move from cover to cover.

The Glaring One was easy to spot. There was that owl-like mask, once again gleaming by torchlight. The Siaraili leader never seemed to stray far from his boat. As before, he was arguing with one of his own people. He seemed frustrated by something. At last, as Kannujaq watched, the leader tore off the kannujaq shell over his head—it seemed to be one piece with the mask—and he cast it on the stones of the beach. The Glaring One, as it turned out, was ruddy skinned for one of the Siaraili. But, other than a short, dark beard, Kannujaq could see little of his features.

The Glaring One's hulking servant, the one he had argued with, watched his leader climb back into the boat, searching about until he picked up something near its stern. Then the Glaring One stretched himself out, drinking from what looked like a kind of skin container. If so, the container was much like the sort Kannujaq's own folk might use. Given what Siaq had told him of the Siaraili drinking habits, however, Kannujaq doubted that it held water.

The servant shook his head and left his leader there, joining the other raiders at a fire they had constructed. For fuel, they were burning the precious few driftwood tools the Tuniit had made over generations.

But at least they're eating, Kannujaq noted. The raiders had found the meat, but the poison would take some time to work. Kannujaq needed patience. The kind of patience he required while hunting. Compared with waiting for a seal to surface, however, this wait was easy.

But at least seal hunting was sane. Kannujaq could still not believe that he was doing this. If the poison failed, or if the giant-men spotted him . . .

For now, it seemed that the Glaring One's men were cocky, overconfident, too used to their raids going smoothly. They had not even bothered to post a lookout. Kannujaq sighed to himself, pleased with such luck. If an alarm went up, the entire plan would dissolve like fat in fire. So far, he had not spotted anyone hefting bows and arrows. That, too, was a piece of luck. He doubted that any archery contest between himself and the Siaraili would go as well as his encounter with Angula.

It was a sudden thing when it happened. Kannujaq's breath hissed between his teeth.

The Siaraili were still laughing, but Kannujaq could see that their movements had become funny. Loose. Disjointed. After a few more minutes, whenever one of the raiders arose from sitting, he teetered dangerously, almost staggering into the fire pit.

One of them suddenly vomited. The others laughed at this, crazily, before they did the same. The mad pitch of their laughter increased, until they fell. First, they were on their knees. Then, they started to fall on their sides. Most began gesturing. Calling out at empty air.

In time, all eight of the raiders were down. Some were shaking violently, like a sleeper having nightmares. One lay still. Others were laughing or weeping uncontrollably.

Jerky from his own nerves, Kannujaq unravelled a bull-roarer that he carried in hand. The object was a small bone that could be found inside a caribou's hoof. When attached to a cord about arm's length, it could be whirled round and round. The resultant noise was a low-pitched buzz, useful for sending a signal.

Feeling that, even now, it was a bit of a risk to abandon his crouch, Kannujaq paused for a long moment, watching his fingers tremble. Then he cursed himself as a coward, forced his legs and back straight. He whirled the bull-roarer with all his strength. The caribou bone hummed, singing on the air.

He was calling the Tuniit.

Now! Now! Kannujaq thought, almost panicking when none of the Tuniit appeared. *I can't do this alone!*

But how could he expect the Tuniit to be any less terrified than himself?

At last, Tuniit men appeared next to him, long bear-spears in hand. They stood stunned by what they saw of the fallen raiders. Kannujaq roared at them to get moving.

He did not watch as they stabbed the giant-men.

Kannujaq's objective was the boat. Hissing aloud like some mad angakkuq, he ordered several Tuniit men to join him and do as he did.

Kannujaq flew down toward the water, almost leaping, almost stumbling, head forward, when his legs seemed incapable of running fast enough. At the water's edge, he threw himself against the bow of the boat. The Tuniit men did likewise. Together, they began to shove the great loon-wolf-thing backward, until even the waterproof stitches of Kannujaq's boots were useless, as the seawater's biting cold surrounded his legs. Still, Kannujaq and the Tuniit heaved, and the huge boat did move.

Kannujaq's one great worry was the Glaring One himself. He had hoped that the man would join his fellows in feasting. He'd been wrong. Instead, the Glaring One seemed to have gone to sleep in the stern. Siaq and Siku had both insisted that the weird fluid the giant-men liked to drink made them sluggish, but still violent. Could they get the boat away from the beach before the Glaring One woke up?

Keep on sleeping, Kannujaq thought toward the Glaring One as he heaved. *Just sleep . . .*

But there was a sudden, dry, rasping sound—that of a weapon being drawn—and the Glaring One appeared with a bellow. Kannujaq barely fell away from the boat as a great blade bit into the wood near his face.

The Tuniit, however, at last found their courage. No longer fleeing like frightened caribou, they came together as a team, and put their powerful shoulders into one last heave. By the time they managed to push the loon-wolf-boat away from the beach, all stood up to their thighs in the frigid water, Kannujaq included. They splashed and waded back up onto the beach, shivering from a combination of cold and nervous tension. Kannujaq was the first to turn, to look back and see if the Glaring One dared to climb out of his boat.

He did not.

Kannujaq and the Tuniit watched from the shore,

panting, shivering. Other Tuniit, with reddened spears in hand, came to stand with them. Kannujaq assumed that they had finished off the Glaring One's servants. Now, there remained only the leader himself, unmasked, staring at them all as his boat drifted further out into the water. Kannujaq opened his mouth to tell the Tuniit to fetch bows, but one glance told him that they were already sickened by the violence they had committed. He disliked the fact that he, himself, was still ready to kill; and he realized that the desire was born only out of his terror. His fatigue. His fear that a threat still remained.

The Tuniit were right. He heard the rattle of spears from men dropping their weapons, as though they had become poisonous to touch, on the stones of the beach.

Kannujaq stared at the Glaring One, now no longer needing to flinch or hide before the other's gaze. They had killed him, anyway. In a sense. There was no way that a single man could handle such a large boat.

The Glaring One returned Kannujaq's stare, his face calm, as though he understood his fate and the fact that there was no longer any need to rage. Currents were already tugging at the boat, turning and drawing it away from the coast. There stood the Glaring One, no longer glaring, but only watching Kannujaq with a hint of sadness. It was a strange thing that there was no hatred in those ice-blue eyes. Only despair and acceptance.

Suddenly, Kannujaq recognized the colour of those eyes. He had seen that kind of ice-blue before.

Then Kannujaq understood.

The Glaring One had never come here for his kannujaq weapons and tools. He was seeking a different kind of treasure. Siaq, the mother of Siku, had kept a secret from them all.

In a heartbeat, it all made sense to Kannujaq: The Glaring One was a wealthy man. He and his servants

had always owned enough weapons and tools. The objects that Angula had stolen meant nothing to them. As with Kannujaq's own folk, what mattered most to the Glaring One was family. Kin. Kannujaq realized, in that moment, that he was looking at a fellow stranger in these lands. A newcomer. One who has known the dread, but also the delight, of the unknown Land. For the first time, Kannujaq found himself wondering what the Glaring One's people were like. Really like. Maybe they had more in common with Kannujaq's folk than he had wanted to admit. Maybe they had just arrived in this area, or nearby. Maybe they had not done as well, in surviving the Land, as Kannujaq's people.

The Glaring One, Kannujaq realized, was a man whose sole treasure had become family. Perhaps his greatest fear was that he and his kind would die alone, without generations to succeed them, on the uncaring Land. After all, everyone wanted to matter. To count. To place some mark on the world that said, "Remember me. I was here." Even if it were only in the memories of children and grandchildren. Kannujaq knew, now, that the leader of the raiders had not come all this way, time and again, just to harass the poor Tuniit. That had been the men—frustrated and angry at being ordered to a place where they did not want to go. To search for a child who was not their own.

The Glaring One's child.

The son he had had with Siaq.

Siku.

12

The Inuit

You've already heard of how Kannujaq and the Tuniit were sick of violence. Imagine how we felt, having to describe it! There were no police in Kannujaq's time and place. No real laws. So, in order for folks to avoid violence toward each other, they often had to *learn* why violence is not a good thing. They had to understand it for themselves, so that when those who had learned the lesson became Elders, they could pass it down to future generations. The Land has a great deal of wisdom to give us, but it's never free.

So, if you see what we mean, you'll find it understandable that there was no real celebration over the defeat of the raiders. The Tuniit simply wanted to put it all behind them. They wanted to return, as soon as possible, to their shy, boring, Tuniit ways.

After all that had happened, Kannujaq did not blame them one bit.

As for Kannujaq's knowledge of Siku, Siaq, the Glaring One, and how all three were related, he didn't bother to speak of it. Why run around, exciting things further by talking about Siaq's husband from beyond the sea? Better to let the Tuniit continue thinking that Siku's blue eyes were supernatural—the mark of an angakkuq, rather than simply the eyes of his father.

In time, Kannujaq offered to bring Siaq and Siku away with him, so that the woman might again know the company of her "dogsledder" folk, and the boy might learn of his ancestors. Half of them, at least.

Siaq just smiled and refused the offer. She was now a Tuniq, she explained. She wanted simple peace. Forgetfulness. And so she would stay.

Yet Siku, in his odd way, went into a three-day seclusion to consider Kannujaq's offer. And it was just as Kannujaq had come to believe that the boy was uninterested that the young shaman suddenly approached Kannujaq, talking as though going with Kannujaq were the most natural thing in the world. Unlike his mother, it seemed that Siku had never felt comfortable among the Tuniit. And he loved the idea of sledding. Just as long as Kannujaq promised that the dogs would not try to eat him.

So, in the early evening, when the little remaining snow was cooling, Kannujaq and Siku got ready to depart. And as Siku watched Kannujaq tighten the lashings on his sled, the boy grew more and more quiet. Almost sullen. As though he were thinking very hard about some disturbing fact.

"*Qanuippit*? Anything wrong?" Kannujaq asked him, finishing a knot.

Siku did not answer for a long moment. Then he sighed, saying,

"I know I'm not a Tuniq. Neither is my mother. We're like you, the dogsledding ones. But what do you call yourselves? What do I call myself, now?"

Kannujaq stood straight, thinking for a moment, trying not to feel anger toward Siku's mother, who had

hurt so many by keeping so much. For the hundredth time, Kannujaq thought:

He's been cheated by his mother. What's a parent for, if not to teach?

It was not Kannujaq's place to speak of Siku's father, but he could at least tell him,

"I've heard my family say that we're just The Living Ones Who Are Here. In the way of our people's talk, they say Inuit."

The word was strange to the shaman boy, and Kannujaq smiled as he repeated it over and over again.

But Kannujaq's smile faded when he thought of Siku's father. The Glaring One's folk.

For the first time, Kannujaq began to worry for the fate of his own people. In his mind, he could not keep himself from comparing them to those he had just fought against. Were his family and all their relations destined to struggle as hard as the Glaring One and his folk? Was it the destiny of new people, in this odd part of the Land, to fade and die? Maybe these ideas were all in Kannujaq's dark imagination. But maybe, in some future time, Kannujaq's folk would exist only in the stories of Tuniit.

Kannujaq was wrong, of course. Oh, his guess about the Glaring One's people was right—the colony from which the so-called giants had come did not end up doing well at all. You might know it, in your time, as the Viking colony of Greenland. Just as you'd call Kannujaq's area Baffin Island. If you could talk to Kannujaq, you might at least offer him some comfort. You could tell him that he was being paranoid. That his own people were destined to travel freely over the next three centuries. That they settled the Arctic. Not only Greenland, but all the lands where the Tuniit had once lived.

But that's where you'd sadden him a bit. Because you'd have to explain that there were no Tuniit in your world. Not all of us make it, you see, especially with so many people pushing at each other on the Land. And Kannujaq's folk would remember the poor, shy Tuniit only in their own stories. In a sense, you might say that Kannujaq's story was of the moment when his world had started to turn into yours.

Kannujaq had worked hard enough. He had been brave enough. Why make his head spin with tales of the future? Besides, at the particular moment where we left him, he was busy concentrating. If you must poke into his life again, you might as well know: Kannujaq was trying to make sure that Siku did not pay too much attention to how he packed his equipment onto the sled.

Why? Well, please remember that Siku was an angakkuq. The boy was pretty insistent that Angula's old treasures had been the source of trouble among the Tuniit. Even the stuff left from the latest raiders was a danger. Basically, the boy was convinced that every remaining tool or weapon equalled sheer evil.

The Tuniit were all in agreement with their camp's shaman. So, nobody made the slightest move to stop Siku when he tossed the treasure, in nine great loads, into the sea's freezing embrace. Kannujaq didn't help. But he watched, whimpering a bit, as the stuff was hurled from a cliff, into deep water. Forever.

By now, Kannujaq had not only come to know that the Tuniit were human beings. He had also come to respect them. He respected Siku, as well. He even liked him. So, he hoped that the young shaman would not be too upset when he at last discovered that Kannujaq had kept a knife. It was the one that Angula had carried. Kannujaq had found it at the edge of the community, lying forgotten in the snow. It was a small reward, Kannujaq supposed, for his help against the Glaring One. And he could hardly wait to use it for iglu building when the next winter arrived.

Give Kannujaq a break! He's not a Tuniq. Nor are his descendants. To this very day, Inuit are a sensible folk.

Pronunciation Guide

We hope you've liked the story, but it's time to be a drag: We thought we'd let you know what the names and words in Kannujaq's tale actually mean. We also thought that, for those unfamiliar with Inuktitut, we'd give you an idea of Inuktitut pronunciation. Meanings aren't a problem, but pronunciation always sparks a fuss. Inuktitut speakers always want their own dialects presented, their own way of saying things in their region or village, and we just can't provide that.

It's like when a given person says, "You all." Then another person says, "Y'all." Who is right? Well, they both are, from the point of view of their way of speaking. We'd love it, if by some magic, we could present every mode of Inuktitut (writing "Hila" instead of "Sila," for example); but in order to tell a story, we have to pick one way and stick to it.

On top of it all, Inuktitut works best in syllabics, not in the Roman alphabet. So please bear in mind, as you read on, that this guide is very rough; meant to at least give crude sound impressions for throats untrained in Inuktitut pronunciation.

a: "uh" sound, as in "supper"

u: soft "oo," as in "cook"

i: "ih" sound, as in "hitch"

j: "y" sound, as in "yellow"

r: indistinct, pronounced in the back of the throat

q: pronounced in the back of the throat

doubled vowels/consonants: lingering emphasis

Glossary

ANGAKKUQ (pronounced "u-nguk-kooq"; spelled ᐊᖓᑯᖅ in syllabics): This is a shaman, a man or woman (sometimes a child) with magical powers, who can see into the unseen world of magical creatures. Shamans have been important in nearly all cultures of the world, though Inuit have particularly strong and recent memories of their shamanic traditions. Contrary to popular opinion, shamanism was not religious to Inuit; instead, the shaman was something more like a tradesperson. Shamans could use their powers for good or evil, but they were important for their ability to explain or manipulate unseen powers on behalf of ordinary humans.

ANGULA (pronounced "u-ngoo-lu"; spelled ᐊᖑᓚ in syllabics): This word means "to chew on skin or pluck feathers with one's teeth."

INUIT (pronounced "i-noo-eet"; spelled ᐃᓄᐃᑦ in syllabics): The singular of this word is Inuk. While it means "Persons," it more literally means "The Living Ones Who Are Here." Its root is inua, the abstract essence of humanness. As what archaeologists term the "Thule" culture, Inuit expanded aggressively across the entire North American and Greenlandic Arctic, between 800 and 1200 C.E. Their origins are Siberian; and, while it is debated as to whether or not their expansion represented a search for metals, it is known that they were a brilliantly innovative hunting culture. In their strong oral traditions, Inuit still hold memories of their encounters with the strange "Dorset" culture—or, in the Inuktitut language, Tuniit.

INUKSUIT (pronounced "i-nook-shoo-eet"; spelled ᐃᓄᒃᓱᐃᑦ in syllabics): The singular of this word is inuksuk. This is a pile of rocks, built in the rough form of a human being, positioned on high ground. Inuksuit are thought to have been used by the Tuniit, then by the Inuit, to panic caribou, which made them easier to hunt (i.e., the animals would look up and think that people are surrounding them on the hillsides; in avoiding the "people," the animals would then run straight into an ambush). They also happen to make excellent place markers in the Arctic, so that one can avoid getting lost. It is hard to tell how old a given inuksuk is, since people build them constantly, even to this very day.

ISUMA (pronounced "i-soo-mu"; spelled ᐃᓱᒪ in syllabics): This term denotes the most private or intimate thoughts and feelings particular to an individual. As such, it represents the personal mind of an individual—sacred insofar as the isuma of a person must be respected. While the darker side of isuma is that it may result in egoism, a well-nourished isuma is thought to result in healthy inua, humanness, which enriches the larger society.

KANNUJAQ (pronounced "kun-noo-yuq"; spelled ᑲᓐᓄᔭᖅ in syllabics): This word means "copper." The character Kannujaq is named after copper, a very rare substance known to his people, the Inuit.

NUNA (pronounced "noo-nu"; spelled ᓄᓇ in syllabics): This term means "land," often referred to as "the Land." While the word can specifically refer to the earth under one's feet (even to the plants that grow in it), it is most often used to refer to the material "suchness" of the world; the stuff of material existence. The interrelation of Land, Sea, and Sky are absolutely critical to Inuit traditional thought and storytelling.

NUNAUP SANNGININGA (pronounced "noo-nowp sun-ngi-ni-ngu"; spelled ᓄᓇᐅᑉ ᓴᙱᓂᖓ in syllabics): This means "The Strength of the Land." To the authors' knowledge, this term was coined by the late Gideon Qitsualik; but it is one of many Inuit ways to express the Inuit tendency to believe that the Nuna, the Land, possesses its own distinct power. The substantial "suchness" of the world can echo the thoughts and feelings of humanity, so that one must take care with idle words and will, lest the Land make them real.

QANUIPPIT (pronounced "qu-nwip-pit"; spelled ᖃᓄᐃᑉᐱᑦ in syllabics): This a traditional question-greeting: "Anything wrong?"

QULLIIT (pronounced "qool-leet"; spelled ᖁᓪᓖᑦ in syllabics): The singular of this word is qulliq. This is a lamp carved from soapstone, which burns seal oil at a steady rate. Among Inuit, it was the very heart of the home, essential for reliable warmth and light. Since every married woman owned one and was trained in its use, it was a powerful symbol of womanhood. As a further symbol of family, it was the place where masculine and feminine energies merged—since the wife's lamp burned seal oil brought home by the hunting husband.

SIKU (pronounced "si-koo"; spelled ᓯᑯ in syllabics): This word means "ice." The character Siku is named after ice, because of his unusual blue eyes.

SILA (pronounced "si-lu"; spelled ᓯᓚ in syllabics): This term means "sky," often referred to as "the Sky." This is one of the most important terms in the Inuktitut language. Alex Spalding's *Inuktitut: A Multi-Dialectal Outline Dictionary* records ninety-six meanings, in senses that are biological, environmental, geographical, locational, psychological, and intellectual. Its most basic meanings include: "air," "atmosphere," "sky," "intellect," "wisdom," "spirit," "earth," "universe," and "all." It has been associated with the pre-colonial concept of a supreme being.

TUNIIT (pronounced "too-neet"; spelled ᑐᓃᑦ in syllabics): The singular of this word is *Tuniq*. The Tuniit are an especially old and mysterious people of the Arctic, pre-dating Kannujaq's folk, the Inuit. In the oral traditions of Inuit, the Tuniit are shy, but very strong. They are thought to have taught Inuit how to live in the Eastern Arctic of North America, having used inuksuit to hunt caribou. By contrast, they lacked many of the more sophisticated tools common to Inuit (e.g., soapstone lamps, toggling harpoons, dogsleds, snow houses, float bladders, waterproof stitching), and their craftsmanship was often thought of as inferior by Inuit standards. They are known to archaeologists as the "Dorset" culture. Historically, the last of the Tuniit are thought to have been the Sadlermiut people of Coats Island and Southampton Island, who contracted plague from sailors in the 1800s; they were extinct by the time the *Active* (a whaling vessel) visited in 1902.

TUURNGAIT (pronounced "too-oor-ngu-it"; spelled ᑑᕐᖓᐃᑦ in syllabics): The singular of this word is tuurngaq. This term really has no decent equivalent in English, though it is often rendered as "spirits." Tuurngait are magical creatures, often (but not always) ethereal and invisible, that can originate from any source. Most are monsters, though some can be animals, plants, people—even rocks. We might call them "subtle" beings of many different sorts. The *angakkuq* often made it his or her habit to have these beings as helpers. Alternately, the angakkuq might remove hostile tuurngait from the community. Tuurngait and shamans were said to have spoken the same secret language, sharing a relationship with the Land's own power.

ULU (pronounced "oo-loo"; spelled ᐅᓗ in syllabics): This is an Inuit woman's traditional crescent-shaped knife. It is like a small axe blade fixed to a short handle (perpendicular to the blade) around which the user's fingers can curl. To this day, the ulu is a common symbol of feminine power (the male symbol being either the straight knife or harpoon head). It is associated with food and, by extension, health. There are Inuit stories of female shamans defeating especially difficult monsters with the throw of a song-empowered ulu.

UMIAQ (pronounced "oo-mi-uq"; spelled ᐅᒥᐊᖅ in syllabics): This is a traditional Inuit skin boat, much larger than a *qajaq* (in English, often spelled "kayak"). The umiaq is able to hold a dozen people on average. The design probably originates in ancient Siberia. Archaeologists assume that it was use of the umiaq, as much as dogsleds, that allowed Inuit and their close cousins to colonize what is now Alaska, Canada, and Greenland, in a relatively short period of time.

About the Authors

Of Inuit ancestry, **Rachel Qitsualik-Tinsley** was born into the traditional 1950's culture of iglu building and dogsledding, later becoming a translator, writer, and activist. She is a scholar of world religions, and considered an authority on Inuit language, mythology, and pre-colonial religion. She has published several hundred articles, as well as many mythic retellings and works of original fiction. Her current projects focus on utilizing fiction to discuss unique Inuit mystical and philosophical concepts stemming from Inuit cosmology of the pre-contact period. Her goal is to reveal, for all readers, the secret thought and sophistication behind Inuit cosmology. She has published for a wide range of ages, her work having been accessed as university course content. In 2012, she received a Queen Elizabeth II Diamond Jubilee Award for her written contributions to Canadian culture.

Of mixed heritage, **Sean Qitsualik-Tinsley** enjoyed a multicultural background steeped in naturalism, before training as a writer in Toronto. He is a literatist of world religions, comparative esoterism, and mythology, having come to focus on Inuit pre-colonial cosmology. After receiving an international award for a speculative fiction short ("Green Angel", 2005), he undertook the task of showcasing the unique flavour of pre-colonial Inuit imagery, combining speculative fiction elements with the world-setting of ancient Inuit thought. He is fascinated by the deep structure and "magical histories" borne in mythical allegory. His fiction and non-fiction, some of which has been accessed as university content, addresses a general range of ages.

INHABIT
MEDIA